Nate the Great
Saves the
King of Sweden

Nate the Great
Saves the
King of Sweden

by Marjorie Weinman Sharmat
illustrated by Marc Simont

A Yearling Book

Published by
Yearling
an imprint of
Random House Children's Books
a division of Random House, Inc.
New York

Visit us on the Web! www.randomhouse.com/kids

**Educators and librarians, for a variety of teaching tools, visit us at
www.randomhouse.com/teachers**

ISBN: 0-440-41302-8

Reprinted by arrangement with Delacorte Press
Printed in the United States of America
One Previous Edition
New Yearling Edition January 2006
20
UPR

This book is dedicated to the
King of Sweden,
who, would you believe,
I do not know,
but I think I would like to know,
provided he is grateful
that I kept Rosamond
from knocking on his palace door.

—M.W.S.

I, Nate the Great, am a detective.
My dog, Sludge, helps me.
I solve easy cases and hard cases.
Sometimes I solve strange cases.
Especially for Rosamond.
But this summer Rosamond was in Scandinavia.
There would not be any strange cases to solve.
That is what I, Nate the Great, thought until I looked in my mailbox.

I found a big picture postcard
from Rosamond.
The picture was of a palace.
So far, so good.
There was a message from
Rosamond.

Dear Nate,
I was in Norway.
Now I am in Sweden.
I was in this palace today.
I did not see the king.
I did not see a detective.
I lost something on my trip.
I don't know where.
I need your help.
If you don't help me,
I will have to ask

the King of Sweden
to take the case.

> *Rosamond*

P.S. What I lost is very tiny
and works only at night.
It lives in dark places.
It looks smart like you
and thinks hard like you
but it has a very long nose
so it probably thinks
through its nose
instead of its head
but I'm not sure about that.

Rosamond was even stranger
in Scandinavia
than she was at home.

I, Nate the Great,
could not take a case
that was thousands
and thousands
and thousands
of miles away.
I threw Rosamond's card
in the wastebasket.

The next day I got another card.

Here are the rules:
If you don't take the case,
call Sweden. Ask for Rosamond.
If you take the case,
you don't have to call.

Rosamond

P.S. If you don't take the case,
I will hire that king.
I will call him up.
I will send him cards.
I will knock on his palace door.
I will get him.

I stared at Rosamond's card.
There was a nice stamp on it.
There was a man's picture on the stamp.

He looked like a king.
He did not look like anyone
who would want to be hired
by Rosamond.
I began to think.
This could be my biggest case yet.
It was international.

Rosamond had lost something
in a foreign country.
Maybe in a palace.
Maybe I could even save
the King of Sweden
from Rosamond.
I wrote a note to my mother.

This case was a big blank.

Rosamond had not sent her address.

I did not know what she lost

or when she lost it

or what country she lost it in.

How could I even begin?

I decided to start at Annie's house.

Annie and Rosamond are good
friends.

Sludge and I went to Annie's house.

Annie was out front

with her dog, Fang.

"I am on a case," I said.

"Rosamond lost something
somewhere in Scandinavia.

What do you know about
her trip?"

"I helped her pack," Annie said.

"What did she pack?" I asked.

"Was it anything that looked smart and had a long nose?"

Fang looked up.

He thought I was talking about him.

Annie said, "Rosamond took
clothes, shoes,
boots for hiking in the mountains,
toothbrush and paste,
a hairbrush,
and toys for her cats."
"Rosamond took her cats to
Scandinavia?"
"Yes, she said that the fish
taste better over there."
"What she lost does not sound like
anything that she packed."
"She packed in a strange way,"
Annie said. "She had a special
place for everything.
She put her left boot
on the left side of her suitcase,

and her right boot on the right side.
She put her cats' toy mice in
her shoes."
"Why?"
"She said her shoes could be
like mice holes for the mice.
Their home. Want to hear more?"
"Not if I can help it," I said.

"Tell me, has Rosamond written
to you?"
"Well, last week I got
this photo from Norway."
Annie pulled a picture
from her pocket.
I looked at it.
I saw Rosamond and her four cats.
They were standing in front
of a store.
It looked like a gift shop.
There were T-shirts and mugs
and little figures
in the store window.
Rosamond and her cats
were all wearing T-shirts.

Printed on every shirt was
NORGE KJERLIGHET ROSAMOND.
I turned the picture over.
On the back Rosamond had written,
"This means Norway Loves
Rosamond."
Annie said, "Rosamond told me
that she was going to buy

T-shirts and have something
printed on them."

"Aha!" I said. "Since Rosamond
didn't lose something she packed,
she must have lost
something she bought.
Do you have her address?"

"No, she keeps moving around."

"May I borrow this picture?"

"Sure," Annie said. "Can you find out
why Norway loves Rosamond?"

"I, Nate the Great, would need
a million years to find one clue."
Sludge and I went home.
I got my magnifying glass.
I looked at the photo
Annie got from Rosamond.

I looked at the little figures
in the store window.
They were trolls.
They had very long noses
and hair like a mop.
Hmmm.

Rosamond had written
that what she lost
looked smart like me
and had a very long nose.
I was getting a clue
that I did not like.
Rosamond had lost a troll.
I, Nate the Great,
do not look, think,
or act like a troll.
Actually I did not know
what trolls thought
or acted like.
But I was pretty sure
that they
were not detectives.

They did not eat pancakes
or have a dog named Sludge.
I needed more clues.
"We must go to the library,"
I said to Sludge.
Sludge had to wait outside.
I looked up Trolls.
There was a lot to read.

Most of it was folklore.
I read that trolls live in the
mountains and caves
and under bridges in Norway.
In dark places,
just like Rosamond had written.
They love to eat
all kinds of berries.
They have dark hair
and they never cut it.

I left the library.
Sludge and I walked home.
I had been right about one thing.
Trolls do not eat pancakes.
But I, Nate the Great, do.
At home I made pancakes.
I gave Sludge a bone.

He ate part of it.
Then he took the rest
in his mouth
and went to the door.
I let him out.
He walked around the yard.
I knew what he was doing.
He was looking for
a special place
to bury the rest of his bone.
I ate my pancakes
and thought about the case.
I knew that Rosamond had lost
a tiny troll.
Did she lose it in the palace?
I needed to know more.
I got Sludge.

"Come," I said, "we must
go to Esmeralda's house.
Esmeralda always knows things."
Esmeralda was in her yard
reading a book.
"Esmeralda," I said,
"I am on a case.
Do you know why someone
would take a troll to a palace?"
Esmeralda didn't blink an eye.
She said, "Is the someone
Rosamond?"
"Yes," I said. "I am looking for clues
about her trip."
"Well, I know she was going
hiking in Norway,
and then shopping for presents.
Then she was going to Sweden.

She wanted to see a palace there."

"In that order?"

"Yes. She was saving the palace
for the last part of her trip."

"Anything else?"

"Along the way she was going to
go to smorgasbords
with her cats."

"Have you heard from her?"
"Yes, she sent me her picture
taken in the palace.
She's holding something
with long, dark hair."
"Aha. Trolls have long, dark hair."
"Here's the picture," Esmeralda said.

"I'm using it for a bookmark."
I looked at the picture.
There was Rosamond in the palace.
And she was holding something
with long, dark hair.
Lots of long, dark hair.
My case was solved!
Rosamond had lost
the troll in the palace.
She had written to me
after she had been
in the palace.
She had the troll there
and then she didn't
have it anymore.
Now all she had to do
was get that troll back.

I, Nate the Great, knew that
when Rosamond came home
I would have to tell her
that she had lost the troll
in the palace.
I knew that she would write a card
to the King of Sweden
and ask him to look for the troll
and send it back.
I knew that Rosamond would write
a very strange card.
I, Nate the Great,
felt sorry for
the King of Sweden.
But a case is a case.
"I have solved my case,"

I said to Esmeralda.
"I never thought
that I would solve a case
in a palace."
I looked at the picture
one more time.
There was something about it.

Something in it.

Something tiny, glittering, and green.

Like a cat's eye.

I looked closer.

It *was* a cat's eye.

Rosamond was not holding the troll.

She was holding one of her cats!

I gave the picture back to Esmeralda.

"My case is not solved," I said.

Sludge and I went home.

Sludge went out
to look for his buried bone.
I watched him look.
He could not find it.
He had not been much help
with this case.
It was time for more pancakes.
And more thinking.
What had I learned?
Was there a clue that I had missed?
I had learned from Annie
how Rosamond packed her suitcase.
I had also learned that Rosamond
bought presents.
And I had figured out that
one was a troll.
And that's what she had lost.

But what if Rosamond
didn't *lose* the troll?
What if she *put* it someplace

and forgot?
Where would Rosamond have
put the presents?

In her suitcase, to bring home.
But Rosamond was moving around,
packing and unpacking.
So if she put the troll in the suitcase,
wouldn't she have seen it?
Now, what had Esmeralda told me?
That Rosamond went

hiking
and shopping
and to the palace
and to smorgasbords.

What was important
and what wasn't?
I heard a scratch.
Sludge was at the door
with his bone.
I let him in.
I looked at him and his bone.

Suddenly I knew
what was important
and what wasn't.
I said to Sludge,
"You were trying to help
with the case
when you went looking
for your bone
in a special place.
You were trying to
tell me something."
Sludge wagged his tail.
I said, "I, Nate the Great,
have just solved this case.
Now all we have to do is
wait for Rosamond
to come home."

Two weeks later
my doorbell rang.
I opened the door.
Rosamond and her cats
were there.
She was carrying her suitcase.

"I'm home!" she shouted.

"I came here first
to tell you that
I am still missing
what I lost.
You are a terrible detective.
I knew I should have hired
the King of Sweden."

"How could I let you know
if I solved your case?"
I asked. "I did not know
where you were in Sweden."

"I'm famous in Scandinavia,"
Rosamond said. "I'm easy to find."

"Open your suitcase," I said.

"Why?" she asked.

"You'll see."

Rosamond opened her suitcase.

"See how neat it is," she said.

"I put everything exactly
where it belongs."

"You packed all the presents
you bought?"

"I got T-shirts and a troll,"

Rosamond said. "I packed
the T-shirts
but I lost the troll.
I thought I had packed it,
but it's not in the suitcase."
I bent down to the suitcase.
I picked up Rosamond's hiking boots.
I looked inside the left one.
It was empty.
I looked inside the right one.
Something was in it.
I reached in
and pulled the something out.
It had the longest nose
and more hair than anything
I had ever seen.

"My troll!" Rosamond cried.
"Now I remember where I put it."
"Yes. Annie told me you had
a plan for everything you packed.
You bought this troll
and you gave it a *home*.
You knew that trolls
live in dark places.

So you put it in
the bottom of your boot."
"Right!" Rosamond said.
"It was cozy and perfect."
"And you forgot," I said.
"You had already gone hiking,
so you didn't use the boots again.
Time went by.
You went to smorgasbords,
you went to Sweden,
you went to a palace.
Then you remembered that
you hadn't seen your troll.
So you thought you had lost it.
I, Nate the Great, say
that sometimes things
are put in places
that are so special

that nobody remembers
where they are.
Sludge had buried a bone
in a special place
and couldn't find it."
Rosamond clutched the troll.
"Oh, you are so lucky
to be such a great detective.
Because now you can have
the present I got you."
Rosamond pushed the troll at me.
"I am giving everyone else
NORWAY LOVES ROSAMOND T-shirts.
But when I saw this troll
in the window,
I knew it was *you*!"
Rosamond closed her suitcase

and walked out with her four cats.
Sludge sniffed the troll.
"This troll still
needs a good home," I said.
I went down to my cellar,
walked to its darkest corner,
and sat the troll down.
"Enjoy your life," I said.
Then I went upstairs.
This case could have ended better
for me, Nate the Great.

But not for the King of Sweden.
He was one lucky king.
He would never get
a card
or a phone call
or a knock on the palace door
from Rosamond.

~Extra~
Fun Activities!

What's Inside

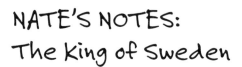

Nate saved the King of Sweden. Who is this guy, anyway? Nate learned a lot about him on the Web.

NATE'S NOTES:
The King of Sweden

The King of Sweden is King Carl XVI Gustaf. His queen is Silvia. They live in Drottningholm Palace. There are eight more royal residences in Sweden.

QUEEN SILVIA AND KING CARL XVI GUSTAF

King Carl and Queen Silvia have three children: Victoria, Carl Philip, and Madeleine.

Here's a neat thing: Traditionally, Prince Carl Philip would have been the next king of Sweden. That's because he's the oldest son of the king and queen. But the Swedish people decided that wasn't fair.

They changed the rules. Now a king's oldest child—boy or girl—becomes the next in line to rule. Result? Princess Victoria will become Queen when her father dies. Too bad for the prince, though!

NATE'S NOTES: Trolls

Nate had a troll in his basement. He thought he should know a thing or two about the long-nosed creatures— just in case. Here's what he found out.

Trolls live in Norway and other Scandinavian countries. (See page 14 for a map of Scandinavia.) Some trolls are big. Some are tiny. All of them are ugly. They have big noses, tough skin, large feet, and messy hair.

Some strange people think trolls are cute. These are the types of people who buy troll dolls. Like Rosamond.

They have good hearing. But they can't see very well.

Trolls are good at smelling things.

They have tails.

Trolls often live under bridges. They sometimes bother travelers who are trying to cross. They demand answers to riddles. They ask for tolls. They sometimes even say they're going to eat the travelers up. "The Three Billy Goats Gruff" is a famous story starring a hungry troll.

Some places are named after trolls. In Sweden, there's Trollhättan, or "Troll's hood." In Fargo, North Dakota, there's a neighborhood called Trollwood.

If exposed to light, trolls are said to turn to stone or explode. But not troll dolls. Too bad.

NATE'S NOTES:
Eating in Scandinavia

Rosamond took her cats to Sweden. She said the fish tastes better there. Does it? Nate wanted to know more. He looked at cookbooks. He learned about eating in Scandinavia.

A smorgasbord is a meal where you can choose from a bunch of different dishes. Some of the dishes are hot. Some are cold.

Often you eat cold fish, like herring, first. Then you might have a plate of Swedish meatballs and noodles.

Smorgasbords often include pancakes. Swedish people eat pancakes with lingonberry jam. Lingonberries taste something like cranberries.

A Map of Scandinavia

Reykjavik

ICELAND

Iceland is a green place with nice weather. The Vikings (seafaring warriors) discovered and named Iceland. The small island country is home to 800 hot springs.

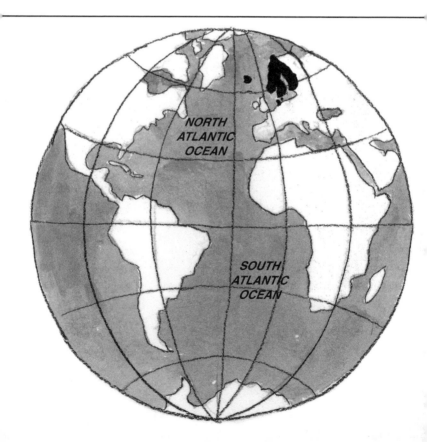

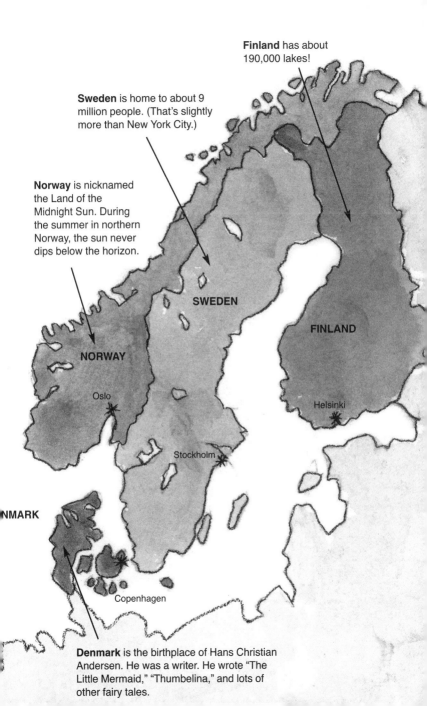

Finland has about 190,000 lakes!

Sweden is home to about 9 million people. (That's slightly more than New York City.)

Norway is nicknamed the Land of the Midnight Sun. During the summer in northern Norway, the sun never dips below the horizon.

SWEDEN

FINLAND

NORWAY

Oslo

Helsinki

Stockholm

NMARK

Copenhagen

Denmark is the birthplace of Hans Christian Andersen. He was a writer. He wrote "The Little Mermaid," "Thumbelina," and lots of other fairy tales.

How to Decorate a T-shirt

Rosamond's T-shirt says NORGE KJERLIGHET ROSAMOND. *That means "Norway loves Rosamond." You can make a T-shirt that says anything you want. Draw pictures. Paint cool designs. Do the King of Sweden's portrait. (Or Nate's.) Try this at a party.*

GET TOGETHER:

- cardboard (cut-up boxes work fine)
- a prewashed T-shirt for each guest
- masking tape
- newspaper
- nontoxic fabric paint
- paintbrushes

DECORATE YOUR T-SHIRT:

1. Slip the cardboard into your T-shirt. Pull the shirt tight over the cardboard. Tape the sleeves and sides to the back.
2. Spread out the newspaper. Place the T-shirt on top.
3. Start decorating! If you like, you can practice your designs on the newspaper first.
4. Let the paint dry. Read the paint bottle to see how long this will take.
5. Wear your shirt with pride. It is one of a kind!

How to Make Swedish Meatballs

The King of Sweden probably eats Swedish meatballs all the time. You should try them, too.

Ask an adult to help you with this recipe.
Makes about 40 meatballs.

GET TOGETHER:

- 1 cup of bread crumbs
- $\frac{1}{3}$ cup of milk
- a mixing bowl
- a skillet
- 1 tablespoon of butter (only if you are also using the onion and garlic)
- $\frac{1}{4}$ cup of chopped onion (if you like it)
- 1 clove of garlic, chopped (if you like it)
- 1 pound of ground meat (Half beef and half pork is good.)

- 2 eggs
- ½ teaspoon of ground nutmeg
- a pinch of salt
- a pinch of black pepper
- a baking sheet
- gravy and noodles
  (See the recipe on pages 24–25.)

MAKE YOUR MEATBALLS:

1. Put the bread crumbs and the milk in the mixing bowl. Let sit about 10 minutes to soften the bread.
2. Place the skillet over medium heat. Add the butter. Melt it. Put in the onion and garlic. Cook about 3 minutes. Let cool.
3. Preheat the oven to 400 degrees.
4. Wash your hands well.

5. Add the meat, onions, garlic, eggs, and spices to the bowl. Mix everything together with your fingers.
6. Shape the mixture into balls about the size of golf balls. Place them on the baking sheet.
7. Bake 12 minutes.
8. Serve with gravy and noodles (recipe follows).

How to Make Gravy and Noodles

Gravy and noodles go well together—and they're even better with meatballs on top.

Ask an adult to help you with this recipe.
Makes four big servings.

GET TOGETHER:

- water
- a big pot
- a skillet
- 1 tablespoon of butter
- 3 tablespoons of flour
- a large spoon
- 1 cup of canned beef broth
- 1 cup of sour cream
- a 1-pound package of egg noodles
- a colander

MAKE YOUR GRAVY AND NOODLES:

1. Add water to the pot until it is about $^2/_3$ full. Place over high heat.
2. While you are waiting for the water to boil, place the skillet over medium heat. Add the butter and let it melt.
3. Add the flour. Stir until there are no lumps.
4. Slowly add the broth. Bring to a boil. Reduce the heat. Add the sour cream. Stir constantly until the gravy gets thick. Remove the skillet from the heat.
5. When the water boils, add the noodles. Read the package to see how long to cook them. Get an adult to drain the noodles.
6. Divide the noodles among four plates. Spoon on the warm gravy. Add the warm meatballs on top. Spoon on more gravy if you like.
7. Eat!

Funny Pages

Knock knock!
Who's there?
Sweden.
Sweden who?
*Sweet and sour chicken
is my favorite dish!*

Q: Where are kings usually crowned?
A: On their heads!

Q: *How do you stop meatballs from drowning?*
A: Put them in gravy boats!

Q: *Why did the troll tell jokes to the mirror?*
A: He wanted to see it crack up.

Q: *Why was herring the easiest dish on the smorgasbord to weigh?*
A: Because it had its own scales!

Knock knock!
Who's there?
Norway.
Norway who?

Norway I'm leaving until you open this door!

Have you helped solve all
Nate the Great's mysteries?

❑ **Nate the Great**: Meet Nate, the great detective, and join him as he uses incredible sleuthing skills to solve his first big case.

❑ **Nate the Great Goes Undercover**: Who— or what—is raiding Oliver's trash every night? Nate bravely hides out in his friend's garbage can to catch the smelly crook.

❑ **Nate the Great and the Lost List**: Nate loves pancakes, but who ever heard of cats eating them? Is a strange recipe at the heart of this mystery?

❑ **Nate the Great and the Phony Clue**: Against ferocious cats, hostile adversaries, and a sly phony clue, Nate struggles to prove that he's still the world's greatest detective.

❑ **Nate the Great and the Sticky Case**: Nate is stuck with his stickiest case yet as he hunts for his friend Claude's valuable stegosaurus stamp.

❑ **Nate the Great and the Missing Key**: Nate isn't afraid to look anywhere—even under the nose of his friend's ferocious dog, Fang—to solve the case of the missing key.

❑ **Nate the Great and the Snowy Trail**: Nate has his work cut out for him when his friend Rosamond loses the birthday present she was going to give him. How can he find the present when Rosamond won't even tell him what it is?

❑ **Nate the Great and the Fishy Prize**: The trophy for the Smartest Pet Contest has disappeared! Will Sludge, Nate's clue-sniffing dog, help solve the case and prove he's worthy of the prize?

❑ **Nate the Great Stalks Stupidweed**: When his friend Oliver loses his special plant, Nate searches high and low. Who knew a little weed could be so tricky?

❑ **Nate the Great and the Boring Beach Bag**: It's no relaxing day at the beach for Nate and his trusty dog, Sludge, as they search through sand and surf for signs of a missing beach bag.

❑ **Nate the Great Goes Down in the Dumps**: Nate discovers that the only way to clean up this case is to visit the town dump. Detective work can sure get dirty!

❑ **Nate the Great and the Halloween Hunt**: It's Halloween, but Nate isn't trick-or-treating for candy. Can any of the witches, pirates, and robots he meets help him find a missing cat?

❑ **Nate the Great and the Musical Note**: Nate is used to looking for clues, not listening for them! When he gets caught in the middle of a musical riddle, can he hear his way out?

❑ **Nate the Great and the Stolen Base**: It's not easy to track down a stolen base, and Nate's hunt leads him to some strange places before he finds himself at bat once more.

❑ **Nate the Great and the Pillowcase**: When a pillowcase goes missing, Nate must venture into the dead of night to search for clues. Everyone sleeps easier knowing Nate the Great is on the case!

❑ **Nate the Great and the Mushy Valentine**: Nate hates mushy stuff. But when someone leaves a big heart taped to Sludge's doghouse, Nate must help his favorite pooch discover his secret admirer.

❑ **Nate the Great and the Tardy Tortoise**: Where did the mysterious green tortoise in Nate's yard come from? Nate needs all his patience to follow this slow . . . slow . . . clue.

❑ **Nate the Great and the Crunchy Christmas**: It's Christmas, and Fang, Annie's scary dog, is not feeling jolly. Can Nate find Fang's crunchy Christmas mail before Fang crunches on *him*?

❑ **Nate the Great Saves the King of Sweden**: Can Nate solve his *first-ever* international case without leaving his own neighborhood?

❑ **Nate the Great and Me: The Case of the Fleeing Fang**: A surprise Happy Detective Day party is great fun for Nate until his friend's dog disappears! Help Nate track down the missing pooch, and learn all the tricks of the trade in a special fun section for aspiring detectives.

❑ **Nate the Great and the Monster Mess**: Nate loves his mother's deliciously spooky Monster Cookies, but the recipe has vanished! This is one case Nate and his growling stomach can't afford to lose.

❑ **Nate the Great, San Francisco Detective**: Nate visits his cousin Olivia Sharp in the big city, but it's no vacation. Can he find a lost joke book in time to save the world?

❑ **Nate the Great and the Big Sniff**: Nate depends on his dog, Sludge, to help him solve all his cases. But Nate is on his own this time, because Sludge has disappeared! Can Nate solve the case and recover his canine buddy?

❑ **Nate the Great on the Owl Express**: Nate boards a train to guard Hoot, his cousin Olivia Sharp's pet owl. Then Hoot vanishes! Can Nate find out *whooo* took the feathered creature?